L.&.D
edition

Mellonta Tauta

Poe, Edgar Allan

Published: 1849

About Poe:

Edgar Allan Poe was an American poet, short story writer, playwright, editor, critic, essayist and one of the leaders of the American Romantic Movement. Best known for his tales of the macabre and mystery, Poe was one of the early American practitioners of the short story and a progenitor of detective fiction and crime fiction. He is also credited with contributing to the emergent science fiction genre.Poe died at the age of 40. The cause of his death is undetermined and has been attributed to alcohol, drugs, cholera, rabies, suicide (although likely to be mistaken with his suicide attempt in the previous year), tuberculosis, heart disease, brain congestion and other agents.

TO THE EDITORS OF THE LADY'S BOOK:

I have the honor of sending you, for your magazine, an article which I hope you will be able to comprehend rather more distinctly than I do myself. It is a translation, by my friend, Martin Van Buren Mavis, (sometimes called the "Toughkeepsie Seer") of an odd-looking MS. which I found, about a year ago, tightly corked up in a jug floating in the Mare Tenebrarum—a sea well described by the Nubian geographer, but seldom visited now-a-days, except for the transcendentalists and divers for crotchets.

Truly yours,
EDGAR A. POE

ON BOARD BALLOON "SKYLARK"

April, 1, 2848

NOW, my dear friend—now, for your sins, you are to suffer the infliction of a long gossiping letter. I tell you distinctly that I am going to punish you for all your impertinences by being as tedious, as discursive, as incoherent and as unsatisfactory as possible. Besides, here I am, cooped up in a dirty balloon, with some one or two hundred of the canaille, all bound on a pleasure excursion, (what a funny idea some people have of pleasure!) and I have no prospect of touching terra firma for a month at least. Nobody to talk to. Nothing to do. When one has nothing to do, then is the time to correspond with ones friends. You perceive, then, why it is that I write you this letter—it is on account of my ennui and your sins.

Get ready your spectacles and make up your mind to be annoyed. I mean to write at you every day during this odious voyage.

Heigho! when will any Invention visit the human pericranium? Are we forever to be doomed to the thousand inconveniences of the balloon? Will nobody contrive a more expeditious mode of progress? The jog-trot movement, to my thinking, is little less than positive torture. Upon my word we have not made more than a hundred miles the hour since leaving home! The very birds beat us—at least some of them. I assure you that I do not exaggerate at all. Our motion, no doubt, seems slower than it actually is—this on account of our having no objects about us by which to estimate our velocity, and on account of our going with the wind. To be sure, whenever we meet a balloon we have a chance of perceiving our rate, and then, I admit, things do not appear so very bad. Accustomed as I am to this mode of travelling, I cannot get over a kind of giddiness whenever a balloon passes us in a current directly overhead. It always seems to me like an immense bird of prey about to pounce upon us and carry us off in its claws. One went over us this morning about sunrise, and so nearly overhead that its drag-rope actually brushed the network suspending our car, and caused us very serious apprehension. Our captain said that if the material of the bag had been the trumpery varnished "silk" of five hundred or a thousand years ago, we should inevitably have been damaged. This silk, as he explained it to me, was a fabric composed of the entrails of a species of earth-worm. The worm was carefully fed on mulberries—kind of fruit resembling a water-melon—and, when sufficiently fat, was crushed in a mill. The paste thus arising was called papyrus in its primary state, and went through a variety of processes until it finally became "silk." Singular to relate, it was once much ad-mired as an article of female dress! Balloons were also very generally constructed from it. A better kind of material, it ap-pears, was subsequently found in the down surrounding the seed-vessels of a plant vulgarly called euphorbium, and at that time botanically termed milk-weed. This latter kind of silk was designated as silk-buckingham, on account of its superior dur-ability, and was usually prepared for use by being varnished with a solution of gum caoutchouc—a substance which in some respects must have resembled the gutta percha now in com-mon use. This caoutchouc was occasionally called Indian rub-ber or rubber of twist, and was no doubt one of the numerous fungi. Never tell me again that I am not at heart an antiquarian.

Talking of drag-ropes—our own, it seems, has this moment knocked a man overboard from one of the small magnetic pro-pellers that swarm in ocean below us—a boat of about six thou-sand tons, and, from all accounts, shamefully crowded. These diminutive barques should be prohibited from carrying more than a definite number of passengers. The man, of course, was not permitted to get on board again, and was soon out of sight, he and his life-preserver. I rejoice, my dear friend, that we live in an age so enlightened that no such a thing as an individual is supposed to exist. It is the mass for which the true Humanity cares. By-the-by, talking of Humanity, do you know that our im-mortal Wiggins is not so original in his views of the Social Condition and so forth, as his contemporaries are inclined to suppose? Pundit assures me that the same ideas were put nearly in the same way, about a thousand years ago, by an Irish philosopher called Furrier, on account of his keeping a re-tail shop for cat peltries and other furs. Pundit knows, you know; there can be no mistake about it. How very wonderfully do we see verified every day, the profound observation of the Hindoo Aries Tottle (as quoted by Pundit)—"Thus must we say that, not once or twice, or a few times, but with almost infinite repetitions, the same opinions come round in a circle among men."

April 2.—Spoke to-day the magnetic cutter in charge of the middle section of floating telegraph wires. I learn that when this species of telegraph was first put into operation by Horse, it was considered quite impossible to convey the wires over sea, but now we are at a loss to comprehend where the difficulty lay! So wags the world. Tempora mutantur—excuse me for quoting the Etruscan. What would we do without the Atalantic telegraph? (Pundit says Atlantic was the ancient adjective.) We lay to a few minutes to ask the cutter some questions, and learned, among other glorious news, that civil war is raging in Africa, while the plague is doing its good work beautifully both in Yurope and Ayesher. Is it not truly remarkable that, before the magnificent light shed upon philosophy by Humanity, the world was accustomed to regard War and Pestilence as calamities? Do you know that prayers were actually offered up in the ancient temples to the end that these evils (!) might not be visited upon mankind? Is it not really difficult to comprehend upon what principle of interest our forefathers acted? Were they so blind as not to perceive that the destruction of a myriad of individuals is only so much positive advantage to the mass!

April 3.—It is really a very fine amusement to ascend the rope-ladder leading to the summit of the balloon-bag, and thence survey the surrounding world. From the car below you know the prospect is not so comprehensive—you can see little vertically. But seated here (where I write this) in the luxuriously-cushioned open piazza of the summit, one can see everything that is going on in all directions. Just now there is quite a crowd of balloons in sight, and they present a very animated appearance, while the air is resonant with the hum of so many millions of human voices. I have heard it asserted that when Yellow or (Pundit will have it) Violet, who is supposed to have been the first aeronaut, maintained the practicability of traversing the atmosphere in all directions, by merely ascending or descending until a favorable current was attained, he was scarcely hearkened to at all by his contemporaries, who looked upon him as merely an ingenious sort of madman, because the philosophers (?) of the day declared the thing impossible. Really now it does seem to me quite unaccountable how any thing so obviously feasible could have escaped the sagacity of the ancient savans. But in all ages the great obstacles to advancement in Art have been opposed by the so-called men of science. To be sure, our men of science are not quite so bigoted as those of old:—oh, I have something so queer to tell you on this topic. Do you know that it is not more than a thousand years ago since the metaphysicians consented to relieve the people of the singular fancy that there existed but two possible roads for the attainment of Truth! Believe it if you can! It appears that long, long ago, in the night of Time, there lived a Turkish philosopher (or Hindoo possibly) called Aries Tottle. This person introduced, or at all events propagated what was termed the deductive or a priori mode of investigation. He started with what he maintained to be axioms or "self-evident truths," and thence proceeded "logically" to results. His greatest disciples were one Neuclid, and one Cant. Well, Aries Tottle flourished supreme until advent of one Hog, surnamed the "Ettrick Shepherd," who preached an entirely different system, which he called the a posteriori or inductive. His plan referred altogether to Sensation. He proceeded by observing, analyzing, and classifying facts-instantiae naturae, as they were affectedly called—into general laws. Aries Tottle's mode, in a word, was based on noumena; Hog's on phenomena. Well, so great was the admiration excited by this latter system that, at its first introduction, Aries Tottle fell into disrepute; but finally he recovered ground and was permitted to divide the realm of Truth with his more modern rival. The savans now maintained the Aristotelian and Baconian roads were the sole possible avenues to knowledge. "Baconian," you must know, was an adjective invented as equivalent to Hog-ian and more euphonious and dignified.

Now, my dear friend, I do assure you, most positively, that I represent this matter fairly, on the soundest authority and you can easily understand how a notion so absurd on its very face must have operated to retard the progress of all true knowledge—which makes its advances almost invariably by intuitive bounds. The ancient idea confined investigations to crawling; and for hundreds of years so great was the infatuation about Hog especially, that a virtual end was put to all thinking, properly so called. No man dared utter a truth to which he felt himself indebted to his Soul alone. It mattered not whether the truth was even demonstrably a truth, for the bullet-headed savans of the time regarded only the road by which he had attained it. They would not even look at the end. "Let us see the means," they cried, "the means!" If, upon investigation of the means, it was found to come under neither the category Aries (that is to say Ram) nor under the category Hog, why then the savans went no farther, but pronounced the "theorist" a fool, and would have nothing to do with him or his truth.

Now, it cannot be maintained, even, that by the crawling system the greatest amount of truth would be attained in any long series of ages, for the repression of imagination was an evil not to be compensated for by any superior certainty in the ancient modes of investigation. The error of these Jurmains, these Vrinch, these Inglitch, and these Amriccans (the latter, by the way, were our own immediate progenitors), was an error quite analogous with that of the wiseacre who fancies that he must necessarily see an object the better the more closely he holds it to his eyes. These people blinded themselves by details. When they proceeded Hoggishly, their "facts" were by no means always facts—a matter of little consequence had it not been for assuming that they were facts and must be facts because they appeared to be such. When they proceeded on the path of the Ram, their course was scarcely as straight as a ram's horn, for they never had an axiom which was an axiom at all. They must have been very blind not to see this, even in their own day; for even in their own day many of the long "established" axioms had been rejected. For example—"Ex nihilo nihil fit"; "a body cannot act where it is not"; "there cannot exist antipodes"; "darkness cannot come out of light"—all these, and a dozen other similar propositions, formerly admitted without hesitation as axioms, were, even at the period of which I speak, seen to be untenable. How absurd in these people, then, to persist in putting faith in "axioms" as immutable bases of Truth! But even out of the mouths of their soundest reasoners it is easy to demonstrate the futility, the impalpability of their axioms in general. Who was the soundest of their logicians? Let me see! I will go and ask Pundit and be back in a minute... . Ah, here we have it! Here is a book written nearly a thousand years ago and lately translated from the Inglitch—which, by the way, appears to have been the rudiment of the Amriccan. Pundit says it is decidedly the cleverest ancient work on its topic, Logic. The author (who was much thought of in his day) was one Miller, or Mill; and we find it recorded of him, as a point of some importance, that he had a mill-horse called Bentham. But let us glance at the treatise!

Ah!—"Ability or inability to conceive," says Mr. Mill, very properly, "is in no case to be received as a criterion of axiomatic truth." What modern in his senses would ever think of disputing this truism? The only wonder with us must be, how it happened that Mr. Mill conceived it necessary even to hint at any thing so obvious. So far good—but let us turn over another paper. What have we here?—"Contradictories cannot both be true—that is, cannot co-exist in nature." Here Mr. Mill means, for example, that a tree must be either a tree or not a tree—that it cannot be at the same time a tree and not a tree. Very well; but I ask him why. His reply is this—and never pretends to be any thing else than this—"Because it is impossible to conceive that contradictories can both be true." But this is no answer at all, by his own showing, for has he not just admitted as a truism that "ability or inability to conceive is in no case to be received as a criterion of axiomatic truth."

Now I do not complain of these ancients so much because their logic is, by their own showing, utterly baseless, worthless and fantastic altogether, as because of their pompous and imbecile proscription of all other roads of Truth, of all other means for its attainment than the two preposterous paths—the one of creeping and the one of crawling—to which they have dared to confine the Soul that loves nothing so well as to soar.

By the by, my dear friend, do you not think it would have puzzled these ancient dogmaticians to have determined by which of their two roads it was that the most important and most sublime of all their truths was, in effect, attained? I mean the truth of Gravitation. Newton owed it to Kepler. Kepler admitted that his three laws were guessed at—these three laws of all laws which led the great Inglitch mathematician to his principle, the basis of all physical principle—to go behind which we must enter the Kingdom of Metaphysics. Kepler guessed—that is to say imagined. He was essentially a "theorist"—that word now of so much sanctity, formerly an epithet of contempt. Would it not have puzzled these old moles too, to have explained by which of the two "roads" a cryptographist unriddles a cryptograph of more than usual secrecy, or by which of the two roads Champollion directed mankind to those enduring and almost innumerable truths which resulted from his deciphering the Hieroglyphics.

One word more on this topic and I will be done boring you. Is it not passing strange that, with their eternal prattling about roads to Truth, these bigoted people missed what we now so clearly perceive to be the great highway—that of Consistency? Does it not seem singular how they should have failed to deduce from the works of God the vital fact that a perfect consistency must be an absolute truth! How plain has been our progress since the late announcement of this proposition! Investigation has been taken out of the hands of the ground-moles and given, as a task, to the true and only true thinkers, the men of ardent imagination. These latter theorize. Can you not fancy the shout of scorn with which my words would be received by our progenitors were it possible for them to be now looking over my shoulder? These men, I say, theorize; and their theories are simply corrected, reduced, systematized—cleared, little by little, of their dross of inconsistency—until, finally, a perfect consistency stands apparent which even the most stolid admit, because it is a consistency, to be an absolute and an unquestionable truth.

April 4.—The new gas is doing wonders, in conjunction with the new improvement with gutta percha. How very safe, commodious, manageable, and in every respect convenient are our modern balloons! Here is an immense one approaching us at the rate of at least a hundred and fifty miles an hour. It seems to be crowded with people- perhaps there are three or four hundred passengers—and yet it soars to an elevation of nearly a mile, looking down upon poor us with sovereign contempt. Still a hundred or even two hundred miles an hour is slow travelling after all. Do you remember our flight on the railroad across the Kanadaw continent?—fully three hundred miles the hour—that was travelling. Nothing to be seen though—nothing to be done but flirt, feast and dance in the magnificent saloons. Do you remember what an odd sensation was experienced when, by chance, we caught a glimpse of external objects while the cars were in full flight? Every thing seemed unique—in one mass. For my part, I cannot say but that I preferred the travelling by the slow train of a hundred miles the hour. Here we were permitted to have glass windows—even to have them open—and something like a distinct view of the country was attainable... . Pundit says that the route for the great Kanadaw railroad must have been in some measure marked out about nine hundred years ago! In fact, he goes so far as to assert that actual traces of a road are still discernible—traces referable to a period quite as remote as that mentioned. The track, it appears was double only; ours, you know, has twelve paths; and three or four new ones are in preparation. The ancient rails were very slight, and placed so close together as to be, according to modern notions, quite frivolous, if not dangerous in the extreme. The present width of track—fifty feet—is considered, indeed, scarcely secure enough. For my part, I make no doubt that a track of some sort must have existed in very remote times, as Pundit asserts; for nothing can be clearer, to my mind, than that, at some period—not less than seven centuries ago, certainly—the Northern and Southern Kanadaw continents were united; the Kanawdians, then, would have been driven, by necessity, to a great railroad across the continent.

April 5.—I am almost devoured by ennui. Pundit is the only conversible person on board; and he, poor soul! can speak of nothing but antiquities. He has been occupied all the day in the attempt to convince me that the ancient Amriccans governed themselves!—did ever anybody hear of such an absurdity?—that they existed in a sort of every-man-for-himself confederacy, after the fashion of the "prairie dogs" that we read of in fable. He says that they started with the queerest idea conceivable, viz: that all men are born free and equal—this in the very teeth of the laws of gradation so visibly impressed upon all things both in the moral and physical universe. Every man "voted," as they called it—that is to say meddled with public affairs—until at length, it was discovered that what is everybody's business is nobody's, and that the "Republic" (so the absurd thing was called) was without a government at all. It is related, however, that the first circumstance which disturbed, very particularly, the self-complacency of the philosophers who constructed this "Republic," was the startling discovery that universal suffrage gave opportunity for fraudulent schemes, by means of which any desired number of votes might at any time be polled, without the possibility of prevention or even detection, by any party which should be merely villainous enough not to be ashamed of the fraud. A little reflection upon this discovery sufficed to render evident the consequences, which were that rascality must predominate—in a word, that a republican government could never be any thing but a rascally one. While the philosophers, however, were busied in blushing at their stupidity in not having foreseen these inevitable evils, and intent upon the invention of new theories, the matter was put to an abrupt issue by a fellow of the name of Mob, who took every thing into his own hands and set up a despotism, in comparison with which those of the fabulous Zeros and Hellofagabaluses were respectable and delectable. This Mob (a foreigner, by-the-by), is said to have been the most odious of all men that ever encumbered the earth. He was a giant in stature—insolent, rapacious, filthy, had the gall of a bullock with the heart of a hyena and the brains of a peacock. He died, at length, by dint of his own energies, which exhausted him. Nevertheless, he had his uses, as every thing has, however vile, and taught mankind a lesson which to this day it is in no danger of forgetting—never to run directly contrary to the natural analogies. As for Republicanism, no analogy could be found for it upon the face of the earth—unless we except the case of the "prairie dogs," an exception which seems to demonstrate, if anything, that democracy is a very admirable form of government—for dogs.

April 6.—Last night had a fine view of Alpha Lyrae, whose disk, through our captain's spy-glass, subtends an angle of half a degree, looking very much as our sun does to the naked eye on a misty day. Alpha Lyrae, although so very much larger than our sun, by the by, resembles him closely as regards its spots, its atmosphere, and in many other particulars. It is only within the last century, Pundit tells me, that the binary relation existing between these two orbs began even to be suspected. The evident motion of our system in the heavens was (strange to say!) referred to an orbit about a prodigious star in the centre of the galaxy. About this star, or at all events about a centre of

gravity common to all the globes of the Milky Way and supposed to be near Alcyone in the Pleiades, every one of these
globes was declared to be revolving, our own performing the
circuit in a period of 117,000,000 of years! We, with our
present lights, our vast telescopic improvements, and so forth,
of course find it difficult to comprehend the ground of an idea
such as this. Its first propagator was one Mudler. He was led,
we must presume, to this wild hypothesis by mere analogy in
the first instance; but, this being the case, he should have at
least adhered to analogy in its development. A great central
orb was, in fact, suggested; so far Mudler was consistent. This
central orb, however, dynamically, should have been greater
than all its surrounding orbs taken together. The question
might then have been asked—"Why do we not see it?"- we, especially, who occupy the mid region of the cluster—the very
locality near which, at least, must be situated this inconceivable central sun. The astronomer, perhaps, at this point, took
refuge in the suggestion of non-luminosity; and here analogy
was suddenly let fall. But even admitting the central orb non-
luminous, how did he manage to explain its failure to be
rendered visible by the incalculable host of glorious suns glar-
ing in all directions about it? No doubt what he finally maintained was merely a centre of gravity common to all the revolving orbs—but here again analogy must have been let fall.
Our system revolves, it is true, about a common centre of gravity, but it does this in connection with and in consequence of a
material sun whose mass more than counterbalances the rest
of the system. The mathematical circle is a curve composed of
an infinity of straight lines; but this idea of the circle—this idea
of it which, in regard to all earthly geometry, we consider as
merely the mathematical, in contradistinction from the practical, idea—is, in sober fact, the practical conception which alone
we have any right to entertain in respect to those Titanic
circles with which we have to deal, at least in fancy, when we
suppose our system, with its fellows, revolving about a point in
the centre of the galaxy. Let the most vigorous of human ima-
ginations but attempt to take a single step toward the compre-
hension of a circuit so unutterable! I would scarcely be para-
doxical to say that a flash of lightning itself, travelling forever
upon the circumference of this inconceivable circle, would still

forever be travelling in a straight line. That the path of our sun along such a circumference—that the direction of our system in such an orbit—would, to any human perception, deviate in the slightest degree from a straight line even in a million of years, is a proposition not to be entertained; and yet these ancient astronomers were absolutely cajoled, it appears, into believing that a decisive curvature had become apparent during the brief period of their astronomical history—during the mere point—during the utter nothingness of two or three thousand years! How incomprehensible, that considerations such as this did not at once indicate to them the true state of affairs—that of the binary revolution of our sun and Alpha Lyrae around a common centre of gravity!

April 7.—Continued last night our astronomical amusements. Had a fine view of the five Neptunian asteroids, and watched with much interest the putting up of a huge impost on a couple of lintels in the new temple at Daphnis in the moon. It was amusing to think that creatures so diminutive as the lunarians, and bearing so little resemblance to humanity, yet evinced a mechanical ingenuity so much superior to our own. One finds it difficult, too, to conceive the vast masses which these people handle so easily, to be as light as our own reason tells us they actually are.

April 8.—Eureka! Pundit is in his glory. A balloon from Kanadaw spoke us to-day and threw on board several late papers; they contain some exceedingly curious information relative to Kanawdian or rather Amriccan antiquities. You know, I presume, that laborers have for some months been employed in preparing the ground for a new fountain at Paradise, the Emperor's principal pleasure garden. Paradise, it appears, has been, literally speaking, an island time out of mind- that is to say, its northern boundary was always (as far back as any record extends) a rivulet, or rather a very narrow arm of the sea. This arm was gradually widened until it attained its present breadth—a mile. The whole length of the island is nine miles; the breadth varies materially. The entire area (so Pundit says) was, about eight hundred years ago, densely packed with houses, some of them twenty stories high; land (for some most unaccountable reason) being considered as especially precious just in this vicinity. The disastrous earthquake, however, of the year 2050, so totally uprooted and overwhelmed the town (for it was almost too large to be called a village) that the most indefatigable of our antiquarians have never yet been able to obtain from the site any sufficient data (in the shape of coins, medals or inscriptions) wherewith to build up even the ghost of a theory concerning the manners, customs, &c., &c., &c., of the aboriginal inhabitants. Nearly all that we have hitherto known of them is, that they were a portion of the Knickerbocker tribe of savages infesting the continent at its first discovery by Recorder Riker, a knight of the Golden Fleece. They were by no means uncivilized, however, but cultivated various arts and even sciences after a fashion of their own. It is related of them that they were acute in many respects, but were oddly afflicted with monomania for building what, in the ancient Amriccan, was denominated "churches"- a kind of pagoda instituted for the worship of two idols that went by the names of Wealth and Fashion. In the end, it is said, the island became, nine tenths of it, church. The women, too, it appears, were oddly deformed by a natural protuberance of the region just below the small of the back—although, most unaccountably, this deformity was looked upon altogether in the light of a beauty. One or two pictures of these singular women have in fact, been miraculously preserved. They look very odd, very—like something between a turkey-cock and a dromedary.

Well, these few details are nearly all that have descended to us respecting the ancient Knickerbockers. It seems, however, that while digging in the centre of the emperors garden, (which, you know, covers the whole island), some of the workmen unearthed a cubical and evidently chiseled block of granite, weighing several hundred pounds. It was in good preservation, having received, apparently, little injury from the convulsion which entombed it. On one of its surfaces was a marble slab with (only think of it!) an inscription- a legible inscription. Pundit is in ecstacies. Upon detaching the slab, a cavity appeared, containing a leaden box filled with various coins, a long scroll of names, several documents which appear to resemble newspapers, with other matters of intense interest to the antiquarian! There can be no doubt that all these are genuine Amriccan relics belonging to the tribe called Knickerbocker. The papers thrown on board our balloon are filled with fac-similes of the coins, MSS., typography, &c., &c. I copy for your amusement the Knickerbocker inscription on the marble slab:-

This Corner Stone of a Monument to
The Memory of
GEORGE WASHINGTON
Was Laid With Appropriate Ceremonies
on the
19th Day of October, 1847
The Anniversary of the Surrender of
Lord Cornwallis
to General Washington at Yorktown
A. D. 1781
Under the Auspices of the
Washington Monument Association of
the City of New York

This, as I give it, is a verbatim translation done by Pundit himself, so there can be no mistake about it. From the few words thus preserved, we glean several important items of knowledge, not the least interesting of which is the fact that a thousand years ago actual monuments had fAllan into disuse—as was all very proper—the people contenting themselves, as we do now, with a mere indication of the design to erect a monument at some future time; a corner-stone being cautiously laid by itself "solitary and alone" (excuse me for quoting the great American poet Benton!), as a guarantee of the magnanimous intention. We ascertain, too, very distinctly, from this admirable inscription, the how as well as the where and the what, of the great surrender in question. As to the where, it was Yorktown (wherever that was), and as to the what, it was General Cornwallis (no doubt some wealthy dealer in corn). He was surrendered. The inscription commemorates the surrender of—what? why, "of Lord Cornwallis." The only question is what could the savages wish him surrendered for. But when we remember that these savages were undoubtedly cannibals, we are led to the conclusion that they intended him for sausage. As to the how of the surrender, no language can be more explicit. Lord Cornwallis was surrendered (for sausage) "under the auspices of the Washington Monument Association"—no doubt a charitable institution for the depositing of corner-stones.—But, Heaven bless me! what is the matter? Ah, I see—the balloon has collapsed, and we shall have a tumble into the sea. I have, therefore, only time enough to add that, from a hasty inspection of the fac-similes of newspapers, &c., &c., I find that the great men in those days among the Amriccans, were one John, a smith, and one Zacchary, a tailor.

Good-bye, until I see you again. Whether you ever get this letter or not is point of little importance, as I write altogether for my own amusement. I shall cork the MS. up in a bottle, however, and throw it into the sea.

Yours everlastingly, PUNDITA.

Biography & Bibliography

Edgar Allan Poe

Edgar Allan Poe (born Edgar Poe; January 19, 1809 – October 7, 1849) was an American writer, editor, and literary critic. Poe is best known for his poetry and short stories, particularly his tales of mystery and the macabre. He is widely regarded as a central figure of Romanticism in the United States and American literature as a whole, and he was one of the country's earliest practitioners of the short story. Poe is generally considered the inventor of the detective fiction genre and is further credited with contributing to the emerging genre of science fiction. He was the first well-known American writer to try to earn a living through writing alone, resulting in a financially difficult life and career.

Poe was born in Boston, the second child of two actors. His father abandoned the family in 1810, and his mother died the following year. Thus orphaned, the child was taken in by John and Frances Allan of Richmond, Virginia. They never formally adopted him, but Poe was with them well into young adulthood. Tension developed later as John Allan and Edgar repeatedly clashed over debts, including those incurred by gambling, and the cost of secondary education for the young man. Poe attended the University of Virginia for one semester but left due to lack of money. Poe quarreled with Allan over the funds for his education and enlisted in the Army in 1827 under an assumed name. It was at this time that his publishing career began, albeit humbly, with the anonymous collection Tamerlane and Other Poems (1827), credited only to "a Bostonian". With the death of Frances Allan in 1829, Poe and Allan reached a temporary rapprochement. However, Poe later failed as an officer cadet at West Point, declaring a firm wish to be a poet and writer, and he ultimately parted ways with John Allan.

Poe switched his focus to prose and spent the next several years working for literary journals and periodicals, becoming known for his own style of literary criticism. His work forced him to move among several cities, including Baltimore, Philadelphia, and New York City. In Richmond in 1836, he married Virginia Clemm, his 13-year-old cousin. In January 1845, Poe published his poem "The Raven" to instant success. His wife died of tuberculosis two years after its publication. For years, he had been planning to produce his own journal The Penn (later renamed The Stylus), though he died before it could be produced. Poe died in Baltimore on October 7, 1849, at age 40; the cause of his death is unknown and has been variously attributed to alcohol, brain congestion, cholera, drugs, heart disease, rabies, suicide, tuberculosis, and other agents.

Poe and his works influenced literature in the United States and around the world, as well as in specialized fields such as cosmology and cryptography. Poe and his work appear throughout popular culture in literature, music, films, and television. A number of his homes are dedicated museums today. The Mystery Writers of America present an annual award known as the Edgar Award for distinguished work in the mystery genre.

Life and career

Early life

He was born Edgar Poe in Boston on January 19, 1809, the second child of English-born actress Elizabeth Arnold Hopkins Poe and actor David Poe Jr.. He had an elder brother William Henry Leonard Poe, and a younger sister Rosalie Poe. Their grandfather David Poe Sr. had emigrated from County Cavan, Ireland, to America around the year 1750. Edgar may have been named after a character in William Shakespeare's King Lear, a play that the couple were performing in 1809. His father abandoned their family in 1810, and his mother died a year later from consumption (pulmonary tuberculosis). Poe was then taken into the home of John Allan, a successful Scottish merchant in Richmond, Virginia who dealt in a variety of goods, including tobacco, cloth, wheat, tombstones, and slaves. The Allans served as a foster family and gave him the name "Edgar Allan Poe", though they never formally adopted him.

The Allan family had Poe baptized in the Episcopal Church in 1812. John Allan alternately spoiled and aggressively disciplined his foster son. The family sailed to Britain in 1815, and Poe attended the grammar school for a short period in Irvine, Scotland (where John Allan was born) before rejoining the family in London in 1816. There he studied at a boarding school in Chelsea until summer 1817. He was subsequently entered at the Reverend John Bransby's Manor House School at Stoke Newington, then a suburb 4 miles (6.4 km) north of London.

Poe moved with the Allans back to Richmond, Virginia in 1820. In 1824, Poe served as the lieutenant of the Richmond youth honor guard as Richmond celebrated the visit of the Marquis de Lafayette. In March 1825, John Allan's uncle and business benefactor William Galt, said to be one of the wealthiest men in Richmond, died, leaving Allan several acres of real estate. The inheritance was estimated at $750,000. By summer 1825, Allan celebrated his expansive wealth by purchasing a two-story brick home named Moldavia.

Poe may have become engaged to Sarah Elmira Royster before he registered at the one-year-old University of Virginia in February 1826 to study ancient and modern languages. The university, in its infancy, was established on the ideals of its founder Thomas Jefferson. It had strict rules against gambling, horses, guns, tobacco, and alcohol, but these rules were generally ignored. Jefferson had enacted a system of student self-government, allowing students to choose their own studies, make their own arrangements for boarding, and report all wrongdoing to the faculty. The unique system was still in chaos, and there was a high dropout rate. During his time there, Poe lost touch with Royster and also became estranged from his foster father over gambling debts. Poe claimed that Allan had not given him sufficient money to register for classes, purchase texts, and procure and furnish a dormitory. Allan did send additional money and clothes, but Poe's debts increased. Poe gave up on the university after a year, but did not feel welcome returning to Richmond, especially when he learned that his sweetheart Royster had married Alexander Shelton. He traveled to Boston in April 1827, sustaining himself with odd jobs as a clerk and newspaper writer. At some point, he started using the pseudonym Henri Le Rennet.

Military career

Poe was unable to support himself, so he enlisted in the United States Army as a private on May 27, 1827, using the name "Edgar A. Perry". He claimed that he was 22 years old even though he was 18. He first served at Fort Independence in Boston Harbor for five dollars a month. That same year, he released his first book, a 40-page collection of poetry titled Tamerlane and Other Poems, attributed with the byline "by a Bostonian". Only 50 copies were printed, and the book received virtually no attention. Poe's regiment was posted to Fort Moultrie in Charleston, South Carolina and traveled by ship on the brig Waltham on November 8, 1827. Poe was promoted to "artificer", an enlisted tradesman who prepared shells for artillery, and had his monthly pay doubled. He served for two years and attained the rank of Sergeant Major for Artillery (the highest rank that a noncommissioned officer could achieve); he then sought to end his five-year enlistment early. He revealed his real name and his circumstances to his commanding officer, Lieutenant Howard. Howard would only allow Poe to be discharged if he reconciled with John Allan and wrote a letter to Allan, who was unsympathetic. Several months passed and pleas to Allan were ignored; Allan may not have written to Poe even to make him aware of his foster mother's illness. Frances Allan died on February 28, 1829, and Poe visited the day after her burial. Perhaps softened by his wife's death, John Allan agreed to support Poe's attempt to be discharged in order to receive an appointment to the United States Military Academy at West Point.

Poe finally was discharged on April 15, 1829, after securing a replacement to finish his enlisted term for him. Before entering West Point, Poe moved back to Baltimore for a time to stay with his widowed aunt Maria Clemm, her daughter Virginia Eliza Clemm (Poe's first cousin), his brother Henry, and his invalid grandmother Elizabeth Cairnes Poe. Meanwhile, Poe published his second book Al Aaraaf, Tamerlane and Minor Poems in Baltimore in 1829.

Poe traveled to West Point and matriculated as a cadet on July 1, 1830. In October 1830, John Allan married his second wife Louisa Patterson. The marriage and bitter quarrels with Poe over the children born to Allan out of affairs led to the foster father finally disowning Poe. Poe decided to leave West Point by purposely getting court-martialed. On February 8, 1831, he was tried for gross neglect of duty and disobedience of orders for refusing to attend formations, classes, or church. Poe tactically pleaded not guilty to induce dismissal, knowing that he would be found guilty.

He left for New York in February 1831 and released a third volume of poems, simply titled Poems. The book was financed with help from his fellow cadets at West Point, many of whom donated 75 cents to the cause, raising a total of $170. They may have been expecting verses similar to the satirical ones that Poe had been writing about commanding officers. It was printed by Elam Bliss of New York, labeled as "Second Edition," and including a page saying, "To the U.S. Corps of Cadets this volume is respectfully dedicated". The book once again reprinted the long poems "Tamerlane" and "Al Aaraaf" but also six previously unpublished poems, including early versions of "To Helen", "Israfel", and "The City in the Sea". He returned to Baltimore to his aunt, brother, and cousin in March 1831. His elder brother Henry had been in ill health, in part due to problems with alcoholism, and he died on August 1, 1831.

Publishing career

After his brother's death, Poe began more earnest attempts to start his career as a writer. He chose a difficult time in American publishing to do so. He was the first well-known American to try to live by writing alone and was hampered by the lack of an international copyright law. Publishers often produced unauthorized copies of British works rather than paying for new work by Americans. The industry was also particularly hurt by the Panic of 1837. There was a booming growth in American periodicals around this time period, fueled in part by new technology, but many did not last beyond a few issues and publishers often refused to pay their writers, or paid them much later than they promised. Throughout his attempts to live as a writer, Poe repeatedly had to resort to humiliating pleas for money and other assistance.

After his early attempts at poetry, Poe had turned his attention to prose. He placed a few stories with a Philadelphia publication and began work on his only drama Politian. The Baltimore Saturday Visiter awarded Poe a prize in October 1833 for his short story "MS. Found in a Bottle". The story brought him to the attention of John P. Kennedy, a Baltimorean of considerable means. He helped Poe place some of his stories, and introduced him to Thomas W. White, editor of the Southern Literary Messenger in Richmond. Poe became assistant editor of the periodical in August 1835, but was discharged within a few weeks for having been caught drunk by his boss. Returning to Baltimore, Poe obtained a license to marry his cousin Virginia on September 22, 1835, though it is unknown if they were married at that time. He was 26 and she was 13.

He was reinstated by White after promising good behavior, and went back to Richmond with Virginia and her mother. He remained at the Messenger until January 1837. During this period, Poe claimed that its circulation increased from 700 to 3,500. He published several poems, book reviews, critiques, and stories in the paper. On May 16, 1836, he and Virginia Clemm held a Presbyterian wedding ceremony at their Richmond boarding house, with a witness falsely attesting Clemm's age as 21.

The Narrative of Arthur Gordon Pym of Nantucket was published and widely reviewed in 1838. In the summer of 1839, Poe became assistant editor of Burton's Gentleman's Magazine. He published numerous articles, stories, and reviews, enhancing his reputation as a trenchant critic which he had established at the Southern Literary Messenger. Also in 1839, the collection Tales of the Grotesque and Arabesque was published in two volumes, though he made little money from it and it received mixed reviews. Poe left Burton's after about a year and found a position as assistant at Graham's Magazine.

In June 1840, Poe published a prospectus announcing his intentions to start his own journal called The Stylus. Originally, Poe intended to call the journal The Penn, as it would have been based in Philadelphia. In the June 6, 1840 issue of Philadelphia's Saturday Evening Post, Poe bought advertising space for his prospectus: "Prospectus of the Penn Magazine, a Monthly Literary journal to be edited and published in the city of Philadelphia by Edgar A. Poe." The journal was never produced before Poe's death.

Around this time, he attempted to secure a position with the Tyler administration, claiming that he was a member of the Whig Party. He hoped to be appointed to the Custom House in Philadelphia with help from President Tyler's son Robert, an acquaintance of Poe's friend Frederick Thomas. Poe failed to show up for a meeting with Thomas to discuss the appointment in mid-September 1842, claiming to have been sick, though Thomas believed that he had been drunk. Though he was promised an appointment, all positions were filled by others.

One evening in January 1842, Virginia showed the first signs of consumption, now known as tuberculosis, while singing and playing the piano. Poe described it as breaking a blood vessel in her throat. She only partially recovered. Poe began to drink more heavily under the stress of Virginia's illness. He left Graham's and attempted to find a new position, for a time angling for a government post. He returned to New York where he worked briefly at the Evening Mirror before becoming editor of the Broadway Journal and, later, sole owner. There he alienated himself from other writers by publicly accusing Henry Wadsworth Longfellow of plagiarism, though Longfellow never responded. On January 29, 1845, his poem "The Raven" appeared in the Evening Mirror and became a popular sensation. It made Poe a household name almost instantly, though he was paid only $9 for its publication. It was concurrently published in The American Review: A Whig Journal under the pseudonym "Quarles".

The Broadway Journal failed in 1846. Poe moved to a cottage in Fordham, New York, in what is now the Bronx. That home is known today as the "Poe Cottage" on the southeast corner of the Grand Concourse and Kingsbridge Road, where he befriended the Jesuits at St. John's College nearby (now Fordham University). Virginia died there on January 30, 1847. Biographers and critics often suggest that Poe's frequent theme of the "death of a beautiful woman" stems from the repeated loss of women throughout his life, including his wife.

Poe was increasingly unstable after his wife's death. He attempted to court poet Sarah Helen Whitman who lived in Providence, Rhode Island. Their engagement failed, purportedly because of Poe's drinking and erratic behavior. There is also strong evidence that Whitman's mother intervened and did much to derail their relationship. Poe then returned to Richmond and resumed a relationship with his childhood sweetheart Sarah Elmira Royster.

Death

On October 3, 1849, Poe was found delirious on the streets of Baltimore, "in great distress, and... in need of immediate assistance", according to Joseph W. Walker who found him. He was taken to the Washington Medical College where he died on Sunday, October 7, 1849 at 5:00 in the morning. Poe was never coherent long enough to explain how he came to be in his dire condition and, oddly, was wearing clothes that were not his own. He is said to have repeatedly called out the name "Reynolds" on the night before his death, though it is unclear to whom he was referring. Some sources say that Poe's final words were "Lord help my poor soul". All medical records have been lost, including his death certificate.

Newspapers at the time reported Poe's death as "congestion of the brain" or "cerebral inflammation", common euphemisms for deaths from disreputable causes such as alcoholism. The actual cause of death remains a mystery. Speculation has included delirium tremens, heart disease, epilepsy, syphilis, meningeal inflammation, cholera, and rabies. One theory dating from 1872 suggests that cooping was the cause of Poe's death, a form of electoral fraud in which citizens were forced to vote for a particular candidate, sometimes leading to violence and even murder.

Griswold's "Memoir"

The day that Edgar Allan Poe was buried, a long obituary appeared in the New York Tribune signed "Ludwig". It was soon published throughout the country. The piece began, "Edgar Allan Poe is dead. He died in Baltimore the day before yesterday. This announcement will startle many, but few will be grieved by it." "Ludwig" was soon identified as Rufus Wilmot Griswold, an editor, critic, and anthologist who had borne a grudge against Poe since 1842. Griswold somehow became Poe's literary executor and attempted to destroy his enemy's reputation after his death.

Rufus Griswold wrote a biographical article of Poe called "Memoir of the Author", which he included in an 1850 volume of the collected works. Griswold depicted Poe as a depraved, drunken, drug-addled madman and included Poe's letters as evidence. Many of his claims were either lies or distorted half-truths. For example, it is now known that Poe was not a drug addict. Griswold's book was denounced by those who knew Poe well, but it became a popularly accepted one. This occurred in part because it was the only full biography available and was widely reprinted, and in part because readers thrilled at the thought of reading works by an "evil" man. Letters that Griswold presented as proof of this depiction of Poe were later revealed as forgeries.

Literary style and themes

Genres

Poe's best known fiction works are Gothic, a genre that he followed to appease the public taste. His most recurring themes deal with questions of death, including its physical signs, the effects of decomposition, concerns of premature burial, the reanimation of the dead, and mourning. Many of his works are generally considered part of the dark romanticism genre, a literary reaction to transcendentalism which Poe strongly disliked. He referred to followers of the transcendental movement as "Frog-Pondians", after the pond on Boston Common, and ridiculed their writings as "metaphor—run mad," lapsing into "obscurity for obscurity's sake" or "mysticism for mysticism's sake". Poe once wrote in a letter to Thomas Holley Chivers that he did not dislike Transcendentalists, "only the pretenders and sophists among them".

Beyond horror, Poe also wrote satires, humor tales, and hoaxes. For comic effect, he used irony and ludicrous extravagance, often in an attempt to liberate the reader from cultural conformity. "Metzengerstein" is the first story that Poe is known to have published and his first foray into horror, but it was originally intended as a burlesque satirizing the popular genre. Poe also reinvented science fiction, responding in his writing to emerging technologies such as hot air balloons in "The Balloon-Hoax".

Poe wrote much of his work using themes aimed specifically at mass-market tastes. To that end, his fiction often included elements of popular pseudosciences, such as phrenology and physiognomy.

Literary theory

Poe's writing reflects his literary theories, which he presented in his criticism and also in essays such as "The Poetic Principle". He disliked didacticism and allegory, though he believed that meaning in literature should be an undercurrent just beneath the surface. Works with obvious meanings, he wrote, cease to be art. He believed that work of quality should be brief and focus on a specific single effect. To that end, he believed that the writer should carefully calculate every sentiment and idea.

Poe describes his method in writing "The Raven" in the essay "The Philosophy of Composition", and he claims to have strictly followed this method. It has been questioned whether he really followed this system, however. T. S. Eliot said: "It is difficult for us to read that essay without reflecting that if Poe plotted out his poem with such calculation, he might have taken a little more pains over it: the result hardly does credit to the method." Biographer Joseph Wood Krutch described the essay as "a rather highly ingenious exercise in the art of rationalization".

Legacy

Literary influence

During his lifetime, Poe was mostly recognized as a literary critic. Fellow critic James Russell Lowell called him "the most discriminating, philosophical, and fearless critic upon imaginative works who has written in America", suggesting—rhetorically—that he occasionally used prussic acid instead of ink. Poe's caustic reviews earned him the reputation of being a "tomahawk man". A favorite target of Poe's criticism was Boston's acclaimed poet Henry Wadsworth Longfellow, who was often defended by his literary friends in what was later called "The Longfellow War". Poe accused Longfellow of "the heresy of the didactic", writing poetry that was preachy, derivative, and thematically plagiarized. Poe correctly predicted that Longfellow's reputation and style of poetry would decline, concluding, "We grant him high qualities, but deny him the Future".

Poe was also known as a writer of fiction and became one of the first American authors of the 19th century to become more popular in Europe than in the United States. Poe is particularly respected in France, in part due to early translations by Charles Baudelaire. Baudelaire's translations became definitive renditions of Poe's work throughout Europe.

Poe's early detective fiction tales featuring C. Auguste Dupin laid the groundwork for future detectives in literature. Sir Arthur Conan Doyle said, "Each [of Poe's detective stories] is a root from which a whole literature has developed.... Where was the detective story until Poe breathed the breath of life into it?" The Mystery Writers of America have named their awards for excellence in the genre the "Edgars". Poe's work also influenced science fiction, notably Jules Verne, who wrote a sequel to Poe's novel The Narrative of Arthur Gordon Pym of Nantucket called An Antarctic Mystery, also known as The Sphinx of the Ice Fields. Science fiction author H. G. Wells noted, "Pym tells what a very intelligent mind could imagine about the south polar region a century ago." In 2013, The Guardian cited The Narrative of Arthur Gordon Pym of Nantucket as one of the greatest novels ever written in the English language, and noted its influence on later authors such as Henry James, Arthur Conan Doyle, B. Traven, and David Morrell.

Like many famous artists, Poe's works have spawned imitators. One trend among imitators of Poe has been claims by clairvoyants or psychics to be "channeling" poems from Poe's spirit. One of the most notable of these was Lizzie Doten, who published Poems from the Inner Life in 1863, in which she claimed to have "received" new compositions by Poe's spirit. The compositions were re-workings of famous Poe poems such as "The Bells", but which reflected a new, positive outlook.

Even so, Poe has received not only praise, but criticism as well. This is partly because of the negative perception of his personal character and its influence upon his reputation. William Butler Yeats was occasionally critical of Poe and once called him "vulgar". Transcendentalist Ralph Waldo Emerson reacted to "The Raven" by saying, "I see nothing in it",and derisively referred to Poe as "the jingle man". Aldous Huxley wrote that Poe's writing "falls into vulgarity" by being "too poetical"—the equivalent of wearing a diamond ring on every finger.

It is believed that only 12 copies have survived of Poe's first book Tamerlane and Other Poems. In December 2009, one copy sold at Christie's, New York for $662,500, a record price paid for a work of American literature.

Physics and cosmology

Eureka: A Prose Poem, an essay written in 1848, included a cosmological theory that presaged the Big Bang theory by 80 years, as well as the first plausible solution to Olbers' paradox. Poe eschewed the scientific method in Eureka and instead wrote from pure intuition. For this reason, he considered it a work of art, not science, but insisted that it was still true and considered it to be his career masterpiece. Even so, Eureka is full of scientific errors. In particular, Poe's suggestions ignored Newtonian principles regarding the density and rotation of planets.

Cryptography

Poe had a keen interest in cryptography. He had placed a notice of his abilities in the Philadelphia paper Alexander's Weekly (Express) Messenger, inviting submissions of ciphers which he proceeded to solve. In July 1841, Poe had published an essay called "A Few Words on Secret Writing" in Graham's Magazine. Capitalizing on public interest in the topic, he wrote "The Gold-Bug" incorporating ciphers as an essential part of the story. Poe's success with cryptography relied not so much on his deep knowledge of that field (his method was limited to the simple substitution cryptogram) as on his knowledge of the magazine and newspaper culture. His keen analytical abilities, which were so evident in his detective stories, allowed him to see that the general public was largely ignorant of the methods by which a simple substitution cryptogram can be solved, and he used this to his advantage. The sensation that Poe created with his cryptography stunts played a major role in popularizing cryptograms in newspapers and magazines.

Poe had an influence on cryptography beyond increasing public interest during his lifetime. William Friedman, America's foremost cryptologist, was heavily influenced by Poe. Friedman's initial interest in cryptography came from reading "The Gold-Bug" as a child, an interest that he later put to use in deciphering Japan's PURPLE code during World War II.

In popular culture

As a character

The historical Edgar Allan Poe has appeared as a fictionalized character, often representing the "mad genius" or "tormented artist" and exploiting his personal struggles. Many such depictions also blend in with characters from his stories, suggesting that Poe and his characters share identities. Often, fictional depictions of Poe use his mystery-solving skills in such novels as The Poe Shadow by Matthew Pearl.

Preserved homes, landmarks, and museums

No childhood home of Poe is still standing, including the Allan family's Moldavia estate. The oldest standing home in Richmond, the Old Stone House, is in use as the Edgar Allan Poe Museum, though Poe never lived there. The collection includes many items that Poe used during his time with the Allan family, and also features several rare first printings of Poe works. 13 West Range is the dorm room that Poe is believed to have used while studying at the University of Virginia in 1826; it is preserved and available for visits. Its upkeep is now overseen by a group of students and staff known as the Raven Society.

The earliest surviving home in which Poe lived is in Baltimore, preserved as the Edgar Allan Poe House and Museum. Poe is believed to have lived in the home at the age of 23 when he first lived with Maria Clemm and Virginia (as well as his grandmother and possibly his brother William Henry Leonard Poe). It is open to the public and is also the home of the Edgar Allan Poe Society. Of the several homes that Poe, his wife Virginia, and his mother-in-law Maria rented in Philadelphia, only the last house has survived. The Spring Garden home, where the author lived in 1843–1844, is today preserved by the National Park Service as the Edgar Allan Poe National Historic Site. Poe's final home is preserved as the Edgar Allan Poe Cottage in the Bronx.

In Boston, a commemorative plaque on Boylston Street is several blocks away from the actual location of Poe's birth. The house which was his birthplace at 62 Carver Street no longer exists; also, the street has since been renamed "Charles Street South". A "square" at the intersection of Broadway, Fayette, and Carver Streets had once been named in his honor, but it disappeared when the streets were rearranged. In 2009, the intersection of Charles and Boylston Streets (two blocks north of his birthplace) was designated "Edgar Allan Poe Square". In March 2014, fundraising was completed for construction of a permanent memorial sculpture at this location. The winning design by Stefanie Rocknak depicts a life-sized Poe striding against the wind, accompanied by a flying raven; his suitcase lid has fallen open, leaving a "paper trail" of literary works embedded in the sidewalk behind him. The public unveiling on October 5, 2014 was attended by former US poet laureate Robert Pinsky.

Other Poe landmarks include a building in the Upper West Side where Poe temporarily lived when he first moved to New York. A plaque suggests that Poe wrote "The Raven" here. The bar still stands where legend says that Poe was last seen drinking before his death, in Fells Point in Baltimore. The drinking establishment is now known as "The Horse You Came In On", and local lore insists that a ghost whom they call "Edgar" haunts the rooms above.

Poe Toaster

For decades, every January 19, a bottle of cognac and three roses were left at Poe's original grave marker by an unknown visitor affectionately referred to as the "Poe Toaster". On August 15, 2007, Sam Porpora, a former historian at the Westminster Church in Baltimore where Poe is buried, claimed that he had started the tradition in 1949. Porpora said that the tradition began in order to raise money and enhance the profile of the church. His story has not been confirmed, and some details which he gave to the press are factually inaccurate. The Poe Toaster's last appearance was on January 19, 2009, the day of Poe's bicentennial.

Selected list of works

Tales

- "The Black Cat"
- "The Cask of Amontillado"
- "A Descent into the Maelström"
- "The Facts in the Case of M. Valdemar"
- "The Fall of the House of Usher"
- "The Gold-Bug"
- "Hop-Frog"
- "The Imp of the Perverse"
- "Ligeia"
- "The Masque of the Red Death"
- "Morella"
- "The Murders in the Rue Morgue"
- "The Oval Portrait"
- "The Pit and the Pendulum"
- "The Premature Burial"
- "The Purloined Letter"
- "The System of Doctor Tarr and Professor Fether"
- "The Tell-Tale Heart"

Poetry

- "Al Aaraaf"
- "Annabel Lee"
- "The Bells"
- "The City in the Sea"
- "The Conqueror Worm"
- "A Dream Within a Dream"
- "Eldorado"
- "Eulalie"
- "The Haunted Palace"
- "To Helen"
- "Lenore"
- "Tamerlane"
- "The Raven"
- "Ulalume"

Other works

- Politian (1835) – Poe's only play
- The Narrative of Arthur Gordon Pym of Nantucket (1838) – Poe's only complete novel
- "The Balloon-Hoax" (1844) – A journalistic hoax printed as a true story
- "The Philosophy of Composition" (1846) – Essay
- Eureka: A Prose Poem (1848) – Essay
- "The Poetic Principle" (1848) – Essay
- "The Light-House" (1849) – Poe's last incomplete work

L . & . D
edition

Made in the USA
Monee, IL
25 July 2021